THE MINSTREL
—— and the ——
DRAGON PUP

Written by
ROSEMARY SUTCLIFF

Illustrated by
EMMA CHICHESTER CLARK

WALKER BOOKS
LONDON

One spring, a she-dragon made her nest on the edge of a high sea cliff. She laid three beautiful eggs and settled down to sit on them with her tail curled neatly round to keep them all together.

But while she was sitting, a knight on a white horse came riding by. He knew that it was the duty of all good knights to kill any dragons they met with, and so he drew his sword and rode straight at her. But the she-dragon didn't want to fight. Dragons sitting on eggs very seldom do, because the eggs might get trampled on. She only wanted to draw him away from the nest; so she sprang up and went, half flying on her great leathery wings, half running on her scaly hind legs, over the cliff-top grass, with the knight on his white horse galloping after her.

But as she sprang up to run, the tip of the dragon's tail had flicked one of the eggs out of the nest on to the very edge of the cliff.

It was the eldest egg, just ready to hatch, and it hung on the edge for a few moments, rocking to and fro and chirping to itself, and then tipped over and went dropping and hopping and bouncing (dragons' eggs have rather leathery shells) from one grassy ledge to another, all the way down to the beach.

So when the she-dragon, having at last shaken off the knight and his white horse, got back to her nest, there were only two eggs in it. However, dragons cannot count very well, so she never noticed the loss, but settled down quite contentedly on those two.

ne fine spring day – it was the same day on which the she-dragon had lost her egg – a minstrel was walking along the seashore. He was trying to make a new song. Sometimes the minstrel's songs came easily, but sometimes they would not come at all; and then nobody tossed coins into his hat with the broken peacock's feather, and so the minstrel went hungry.

This was a hungry time, and when he found a beautiful egg, creamy white with rose-coloured blotches, among the seaweedy boulders at the foot of the cliff, he did wonder, just for a moment, whether it might be good to eat. But the egg was rocking to and fro and chirping to itself; and as he squatted down for a closer look, a little dark hole appeared, with cracks running from it in all directions.

The egg was hatching!

But with the shell being so tough, whatever was coming out of it was having very hard work. Maybe a little music would encourage it, the minstrel thought, and he began to play his harp to the egg. Just a simple little tune, like a lullaby, but whereas a lullaby is for going to sleep to, this was a tune for waking up to. The thing inside the egg seemed to like it. It wriggled and pushed, chirping more loudly every moment; and suddenly the leathery shell split in half, and out came the oddest little creature the minstrel had ever seen.

It had a green goose-pimply skin and a long tail, and two little flapping things rather like small damp kid gloves that were the promise of wings on its back, and a round pink stomach that, as it dried off in the sunshine, began to be fuzzy with a kind of green swansdown. It was about the size of a kitten.

"I do believe you're a dragon!" said the minstrel, and tickled it very gently under the chin.

Now there are two mistakes that most people make about dragons: they think that they are as big as houses, and they think that they are fire-breathing fierce by nature. Actually they only stand about as high as a Shetland pony when they are full grown, and though they are three times as long, more than half of that is tail. And they are only fierce because their mothers teach them that all humans are dangerous, and knights on white horses are the most dangerous of the breed. And of course this particular dragon pup had no chance to learn anything from his mother. He only knew that he liked the finger tickling under his chin, and he bobbed his head up and down and tried to flap his wings.

"You're hungry," said the minstrel, "and somehow you have lost your mother – or your mother has lost you. You'd best come along with me." And he picked up the little creature and stowed it inside the breast of his tunic, and took it back to his lodging, and gave it some of the milk that he had been going to have with rather stale bread for his own supper.

And so from that day on, the minstrel and the dragon pup – he called it Lucky – went their way together.

The dragon pup never missed its mother, because it had the minstrel. And the minstrel's songs came easily, because he had something to love; which was just as well, because as the dragon pup grew bigger, it took a lot of feeding.

At first the minstrel carried it with him in a bag with three red tassels as he walked from village to village and town to town. But as its legs grew stronger it trotted along beside him, and he made it a collar and lead.

So the time went by and the time went by, and Lucky grew slowly bigger and more beautiful. The goose-pimples on his back turned to polished scales, and the flapping things on his back turned into proper wings, though he did not know quite how to use them yet. His temper was as sweet as an apple, and the thing he liked best in the world was to lie on his back while the minstrel tickled him with the broken peacock's feather from his hat.

Together they saw three springs turn to blue-hazed summer and round through autumn and shivering winter to spring again. And the minstrel made the best songs that ever he had made; and together they were very happy.

ne autumn day when Lucky was about the size of two dachshunds standing end to end, a day when the first leaves were falling and the wind blew cold in their faces, they came to a village. And half-way up the village street was an inn. They went inside, and the minstrel asked for supper and a sleeping place for the night.

Soon word was all round the village that there was a wandering minstrel at the inn, with a real live dragon pup on a lead, just like a dog; and people came flocking in, hoping for a new song, and a sight of the creature.

But with the villagers came a travelling showman. And when he saw the little scaly dragon sitting under the table as good as gold with its supper bowl, he thought what a lot of money he could make if it were his. He would teach it tricks – with a sharp stick to help it learn. People would pay well to see a dragon doing tricks. And if he got tired of trailing the little brute around, he could always sell it for a whole pocketful of silver…

When supper was over, and the minstrel had sung until everybody was happy and he was too tired to sing any more, he untied Lucky's lead from the leg of his stool and took him away to the corner of a disused storeroom where they were to spend the night.

There he took off the little dragon's collar as he always did at bedtime, and rubbed his neck, while Lucky rolled on his back, waving all his paws in the air; and then they both lay down to sleep, well contented, with Lucky at the minstrel's feet.

 The travelling showman lay down before what was left of the inn fire and pretended to go to sleep too. But as soon as the house was quiet, he got up and crept to the kitchen and poked about, looking for the cheese. He had noticed the minstrel giving little bits of his own supper cheese to the dragon. And he had seen how much the dragon pup liked it. At last he found what he was looking for, in a big blue crock. He broke off a lump of the cheese and crept back through the inn to the storeroom where the minstrel and the dragon pup were asleep.

At least somebody was asleep, for putting his ear against the door he could hear snoring, and the snoring sounded human. The door was shut, but when the showman very quietly lifted the latch it opened quite easily. It only needed to open a little way; just enough to let the dragon pup through. And the showman crumbled off a bit of cheese and pushed it inside. The room was so small that it was almost under Lucky's sleeping nose, and the smell of it whispered to him in his dreams.

Stronger and stronger grew the whisper until it woke Lucky up. He got up and nosed towards it; and there it was, a bigger and more beautiful piece of cheese than ever the minstrel had given him! It went down in one gulp.

The showman broke off another bit and put it just in the opening of the doorway. He heard the pup snuffing and the rattle of his claws as he came on towards it. Once, the minstrel stopped snoring. But he was very tired, and he was used to Lucky padding about in the night, so he did not wake up.

The third piece of cheese was well outside the door, and the fourth was half-way across the sanded floor of the inn parlour.

When they were right outside in the lane, the showman, making friendly noises, offered the last bit of cheese. Then he dropped his coat over Lucky's head and snatched him up, half smothering him in the folds before he could let out more than a startled squeal; and set off running, through the sleeping village and away down the lane in the moonlight.

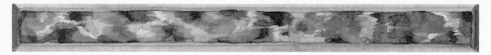

When the minstrel woke up in the morning, there was Lucky's collar and lead lying just where he had put them. But of the dragon pup there was no sign; and the door was not quite shut, though he was sure that he had shut it last night. He asked the landlord of the inn if he had seen or heard anything; but the landlord only shook his head. He searched the inn and the stable yard, whistling and calling; he whistled and called from end to end of the village, asking everyone he met if they had seen his dragon pup. But nobody had.

But one man who had been up late looking after a·sick cow, had seen someone who looked like the showman running down the lane carrying a bundle under his arm. And come to think of it, the bundle had been wriggling a bit; squealing a bit, too.

The minstrel thanked him, and took to the road again, determined to walk all day and all night until he caught up with the showman. But soon the lane branched into three, and there was nothing to tell him which branch to follow. And while he stood

there wondering, a late butterfly hovered past in the sunshine, and danced on down the left-hand lane. The minstrel followed it, there being nothing else to tell him which way to go. But butterflies are not very reliable, and it was the wrong lane.

**T**he minstrel wandered the country with a heavy heart, singing for his supper, rather sadly now, so that his suppers were rather small, and asking as he went, if anyone had seen a man with a bundle that wriggled and squealed, or maybe with a very small dragon on a string.

Once a boy leaning on a gate told him that he had seen someone dragging along a miserable little green monster of some sort on the end of a chain that looked heavy enough to hold a three-masted sailing ship. And once a man making horseshoes told him that he had seen a dragon pup being prodded with a stick to make it sit up and beg. And once an old woman selling laces and ribbons told him that she had seen a bad-tempered looking little scaly creature with a label saying "For Sale" round its neck tied up outside a booth at Blackthorn Fair, but that had been in early spring and now it was high summer.

For the most part, nobody could tell him anything at all.

And the minstrel wandered on and on, his songs getting sadder and his suppers smaller as time went by.

Another winter passed, and it was spring again when the minstrel came to a city. Very busy and very grand it was because it was the Royal City of the country. And on the far side of the city, in a green park shady with trees and shining with water, bright with flowers and loud with bird song, stood the King's Palace, lifting its towers towards the sky.

The minstrel thought that even if the King did not want his songs, maybe the people in the stables or the kitchen would. And in a King's kitchen there might well be some spare supper. So he went up to the main gates, which stood open wide with sentries in blue and scarlet uniforms on either side of them.

"What business have you in the Palace?" demanded one of the sentries, stepping forward.

"I have come to make music for the King," said the minstrel, hoping that he sounded very much better than he felt.

"Well, I dare say he could do with a song to cheer him up," said the sentry. "Pass, friend."

And the minstrel passed. Inside the gates he found the most beautiful gardens all around him, and a broad drive sweeping up between sun-dappled lawns to the front of the Palace.

The minstrel thought that it might be better to go to the back door, because the front entrance, with pillars and statues and flights of marble steps all round it looked so uncomfortably splendid. And so when he found a path turning to the right, he turned off and followed it. And so he came through a belt of flowering trees, to a place where there were several cages grouped together – beautiful cages made of curly wrought ironwork, all light and lacy and painted different colours, with tops shaped like bells and pomegranates and pagodas; but cages, all the same. And in the cages were the most extraordinary creatures: wyverns and griffins and the like, with tails like serpents and heads

and wings like golden eagles, all fiercely splendid, who began to roar and scream and clap their wings and lash their tails as the minstrel went by. There had been a unicorn; but the unicorn had been very unhappy there, and when his cage door had been accidentally left open one feeding time, he had escaped and galloped away.

And in the cage that he had left empty, was a little scaly green thing huddled in the far corner as though it were trying to melt through the bars, its eyes shut and its tail as limp as a bit of string.

Just for a moment the minstrel could not believe it! He had been searching so long, through all the dusty highways and muddy byways of the land, and had almost given up hope. Then he let out a joyful shout, "Lucky!"

The dragon pup looked round, very slowly as though he could not believe it either. Then he jumped up and with squeals of joy came running and hopping across the cage, his tail swinging behind him; and the minstrel squatted down and reached through the bars to greet him.

"And what do you think you're doing?" said a stern voice. And when the minstrel looked round, there stood a fat man with a gold chain round his neck to show that he was the King's Beast-master.

The minstrel scrambled to his feet. "He's mine!" he said. "My dragon! What is he doing here?"

"That's the King's dragon," said the Beast-master. "The King collects strange creatures."

"This dragon is mine! I had him from an egg until someone stole him a year and more ago!" said the minstrel, standing his ground. "Look at him, would he do that if he wasn't mine – if I wasn't his?" For the dragon pup had rolled on his back to be tickled, chirping with delight and still waving his tail.

The Beast-master looked, and he seemed to grow less stern. He was in fact quite a kindly man. "Well, I've certainly never seen him behave like that before. Nasty snappy little thing he's been ever since we bought him at last year's Blackthorn Fair."

"Well of course he has, he's been ill-used and – and unhappy." The minstrel was almost hopping with impatience. "Open the door now and let me have him, and we'll be on our way."

"Not so fast," said the Beast-master. "He's the King's, didn't I say? The King bought him to add to his collection. I can't just give him away!"

The minstrel saw that. "Then I'll go and ask the King."

"I wouldn't," said the Beast-master, "he's got enough to worry him – him and the Queen – with the little Prince so ill and seemingly no one able to cure him."

The minstrel took his thoughts off Lucky for a moment and asked, "What is the matter with the little Prince, then?"

"Nobody knows. It began with a fever, and then he sank into a sort of sleep, but not like a proper sleep. And not all the doctors in the land seem able to waken him."

The minstrel felt a puff of warm breath on the backs of his ankles, and heard Lucky chirping to be noticed. And suddenly he thought of the beautiful egg on the seashore, and the little tune, simple as a lullaby, but for waking up to, not going to sleep to, that he had played to help it hatch. That had been Lucky's tune ever since and he had never played it for anyone else. But now…

"I might be able to wake the little Prince," he said. "Would they let me try?"

"Anyone can try," said the Beast-master.

The minstrel reached between the cage bars and patted Lucky on the head. "Sit!" he said firmly. "Wait! I'll be back."

Then he went on up to the Palace. To the grand front entrance after all because, so said the Beast-master, people coming to cure the little Prince all went in that way.

Inside, everybody had long anxious faces and seemed to be in a hurry. But at last he found a page who didn't seem as anxious or as busy as everybody else, and asked him how to find the little Prince. The page handed him over to a squire, and the squire handed him over to a Gentleman of the Bedchamber, who led him up marble stairways and along colonnades and through halls hung with jewel-coloured tapestries, until he found himself in the Prince's bedchamber.

he little Prince lay on his bed, lost and restless in some kind of uneasy and distressful sleep; with his old nurse wringing her hands, and several grey-bearded doctors talking to each other and shaking their heads in corners. And the King and Queen in their silken robes looking sadly on.

"Not another!" said the King, when the minstrel asked leave to try the power of his waking-up tune.

But the Queen said, "Everybody who comes, must try. Maybe this time…"

So the minstrel tuned his harp and began to play.

He played Lucky's tune over three times very softly. And the first time the Prince's restlessness left him so that he lay quiet and easy; and the second time he breathed a long deep sigh and stretched himself under the embroidered bedclothes; and the third time he sneezed loudly, opened his eyes and looked about him, frowning a little as though puzzled by what he saw.

The minstrel made a quick pattern of notes like a dance of butterflies on a May morning, which he had never made before, even for Lucky.

And the little Prince sat up in bed and said, "That was an odd sort of night! What's everybody doing in my bedroom? I want my dog Pippin and I want my new scarlet trousers and I want brown bread and honey and sausages and a whole bowlful of cherries for breakfast."

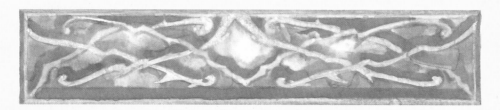

There was a long, dumb-struck silence; and then the rejoicing broke out; and spread until the whole Palace was rocking with it like a belfry rocking with its peal of bells. And in the midst of it all the Queen was crying and the old nurse was scolding

everybody in sight, demanding what they thought they were doing making that uproar in a sick child's bedroom; and the King was pumping the minstrel's hand up and down in gratitude and promising to make him a Lord with a castle all of his own.

But the minstrel didn't want to be a Lord with a castle of his own. "I don't like to stay more than a few days in one place, you see," he explained.

So the King offered him a chest of gold as heavy as himself.

But the minstrel said that such a chest would be very difficult to carry from place to place.

So the King offered him a splendid carriage drawn by four bay horses to carry it.

But the minstrel, thanking him all the same, thought there would be problems about stabling the horses, along the kind of roads he usually followed, and the carriage wheels would be sure to get stuck in the ruts.

"A new harp, then, a harp all of gold, enriched with jewels."

"It wouldn't sound as sweet as my own old harp – which is made of wood, as a harp should be," said the minstrel.

The King was getting hot and bothered. "You have cured my son from his sickness, and I *insist* on expressing my gratitude – a gift in thanks – there must be *something* you would like!"

"I'd like the dragon pup out of your strange beast collection," said the minstrel.

The King took a step backward in astonishment. "That sulky, spiteful little brute? What could you possibly want with that?"

"He's mine, you see." The minstrel drew a long breath to last him while he explained all that needed explaining. "I had him from an egg until somebody stole him, more than a year ago, and I have been looking for him ever since. He's only sulky and spiteful because he's miserable and missing me. So if I can have him back, please, with a paper telling people not to steal him again because he's under your protection, that is what I would really like."

"If that is what you want then that is what you shall have," said the King. "But I don't think the paper will be much good, because if anyone were going to steal him you probably wouldn't have the chance to show it to them first. We must think of a better way."

And he went off to his study, calling for paper and a new quill pen and all the copying-clerks that were in the Palace.

And almost before the little Prince had finished his bread and honey and sausages, Royal Messengers were riding North, South, East and West with copies of the King's proclamation about not stealing Lucky because he and the minstrel were both under the King's personal protection, to be read aloud and pinned up on market crosses in every town and village throughout the land.

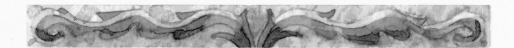

 When the minstrel got back to the cages of the King's collection, he found Lucky standing on his hind legs with his nose poked between the bars, snuffing anxiously and looking for him to come back. The dragon pup broke into a frenzy of chirping and squealing and bobbing up and down as he appeared.

"Aren't you the silly one?" said the minstrel. "Didn't I say I'd be back?" And he took Lucky's collar and lead from his pouch where he had carried them for a year and more.

The Royal Beast-master unlocked the cage door and the dragon pup almost fell out on to the minstrel's feet, and the minstrel squatted down to put his collar on. Lucky had grown quite a lot in the time since he was stolen, but he was so woefully thin that it still fitted him.

It was quite difficult to get the collar on, all the same, because Lucky was so busy rolling and wriggling with delight. But it was on at last.

"Now we're going home," said the minstrel. "Home to the open road, you and I."

And they set off, walking, trotting, almost dancing, down the Palace drive and out through the City and away, following the first road they came to.

The world smelled of sunshine and tree shadows and wayside dust, and

there was a cuckoo calling in the next valley.

The minstrel's head was full of fine new songs to sing, better than ever he had sung before, and Lucky had his friend again and they were both very happy.